MERMICORN ISLAND #3

Too Many Dolphins!

BY JASON JUNE

Scholastic Inc.

To Anna, Priscilla, and Jen,
who are truly mer-mazing

Copyright © 2021 by Jason June

Cover and interior art copyright © 2021 by Lisa Manuzak Wiley

All rights reserved. Published by Scholastic Inc., *Publishers since 1920.* SCHOLASTIC and associated logos are trademarks and/or registered trademarks of Scholastic Inc.

The publisher does not have any control over and does not assume any responsibility for author or third-party websites or their content.

No part of this publication may be reproduced, stored in a retrieval system, or transmitted in any form or by any means, electronic, mechanical, photocopying, recording, or otherwise, without written permission of the publisher. For information regarding permission, write to Scholastic Inc., Attention: Permissions Department, 557 Broadway, New York, NY 10012.

This book is a work of fiction. Names, characters, places, and incidents are either the product of the author's imagination or are used fictitiously, and any resemblance to actual persons, living or dead, business establishments, events, or locales is entirely coincidental.

ISBN 978-1-338-68520-6

10 9 8 7 6 5 4 3 2 1   21 22 23 24 25

Printed in the U.S.A. 40

First printing 2021

Book design by Yaffa Jaskoll

PEARL PROBLEMS

"**HOLY MACKEREL**, Echo!" I said.
"Dolphin pods sure know how to have a
mer-mazing time!"

Echo, Flash, Ruby, and I floated at
the edge of Pufferfish Park. Dozens of
dolphins were swimming and making clam
burgers and playing soccer.

"Thanks, Lucky!" Echo said. "All the

dolphin pods around Mermicorn Island get together every month for **fin and games** like this!"

Flash looked from left to right, taking in the whole park. "This is the most dolphins I've ever seen in my life. There's got to be hundreds of dolphins here.

No! Thousands! Maybe even millions!"

Echo laughed. "Probably not millions, but there's definitely a lot."

"I don't want to show up **empty-hooved**," Ruby said. She squinted her eyes and wiggled her tail, and then red glitter burst from her horn. She was using her Baking Sparkle.

All mermicorns have unique magic that we call Sparkle. Ruby's lets her make baked treats! Other sea creatures in Mermicorn Island have powers too. Seahorses have superspeed, and dolphins have magical echolocation that helps them find anything they're looking for, as long as it's not too small or far away.

"Whew!" Ruby said when ten pink cupcakes appeared in front of her. "I can't make dozens of cupcakes at once yet. Ten is my max. **GIVE ME A minnow,** and I'll be able to make more."

Ruby's words gave me an idea. "Maybe there's a shell in Poseidon's treasure chest that makes **fishies'** magic stronger!"

My SPARKLE hadn't shown up yet, but a powerful mermicorn named Poseidon gave me a treasure chest full of magic shells. I'd found shells that make

fishies invisible, let me speak dogfish, make things grow (sometimes *too* big), and so much more. We call it Shell Sparkle!

"That would help a lot," Ruby said. "Especially with Flash's toy trident."

I could control my magic shells' powers by putting them in Flash's toy trident. It was **mer-mazing**! But if I broke a shell, those powers could get a little **out of hoof,** so I had to be careful.

"We can't just float here all day," Echo said. "Let's go join in the fun!"

Just as we reached the edge of the

soccer field, a dolphin came to the sidelines and blew a whistle around her neck.

"**ATTENTION, PODS!**" she yelled, waving a crab claw clipboard. "I'm here to remind you about tomorrow's Perfect Path Pearl Hunt! Come see me, Dolly Porpon, if you want to sign up."

Dozens of dolphins swarmed Dolly. They looked about as excited as I do when I get a new set of markers. That's really, *really* excited!

"Perfect Path Pearl Hunt?" Ruby asked. "What's that?"

Echo shrugged. "I don't know,"

she said. "Let's go ask my dads."

Echo led the way as we swam
toward her parents, Dalton and Phineas.
They floated near a mermaid selling
milkshakes.

"Dad! Pop!" Echo said. "What's the
Perfect Path Pearl Hunt?"

"It's an event where kid **fishies** look

for eight magic Perfect Path Pearls," Dalton explained. "They show you all the steps you need to take to achieve your biggest goal and get your heart's desire. **Any-fishy** can enter, but dolphins love the challenge. Pearls are so small, it takes extra magic strength to find them with echolocation. It's at the Narwhal Adventure Theme Park."

"That sounds **fin-credible**!" I said. "Our friend Nelia's aunt and uncle made that park." I couldn't wait for the next time she came to visit so we could all go together.

"Ooh, ooh, ooh!" Flash said, bouncing

on his tail. "Can we enter? Please, please, please, please, please?" Flash talks about as fast as he swims, which is *super* fast!

"Yeah! Can we join the hunt?" Echo asked. Her dorsal fin shook again. "It sounds like a **mer-mazing** adventure."

Dalton and Phineas looked at each other. They both had big frowns on their snouts.

"I'm sorry, honey," Phineas said. "Kids need to enter in teams of eight. We were going to surprise you and have your cousins come to town for it. But they all got sick with **fin-fluenza**.

They'll definitely get better, but they can't make it for the pearl hunt."

Echo's frown matched her dads'. "We're only the **Fin-tastic Four**, not eight." She looked to the groups of dolphins signing up. "If I was in a big pod like every other dolphin, I'd have enough pod siblings to enter. I never get to join pod team games because our family's so small."

Dalton and Phineas pulled Echo in for a hug. "We know, sweetie."

Most dolphin families in Mermicorn Island were a part of big groups called pods. But for Echo, it was just her and her dads.

Echo's dads left to get Mermaid Milkshakes to cheer us up.

"I wish I had magic that could make your family bigger," I said to Echo.

"If only we had MULTIPLY SPARKLE like my aunt Mona," Ruby said. "We could multiply you until you had as many dolphins as you want. There'd be enough to have an **eight-fishy** pearl hunt team."

Wait a minnow.

"Maybe we do have MULTIPLY SPARKLE," I said. "Let's check Poseidon's treasure chest!"

DUPLICATE DOLPHINS

Poseidon's treasure chest was at the foot of my bed, and filled my bedroom with a golden glow. My Leonardo da Fishy poster looked **mer-mazing** in the glittery light!

I flipped open the lid. Dozens of sparkly seashells were piled inside.

"I always love looking at these shells,"

Ruby said. "They're so **sea-utiful**. Which one feels right to you, Lucky?"

"Let's see..." I said. I moved my hoof over all the sparkling shells. I usually felt a pull from my mane to my tail toward the shell that would help us the most.

Tingles in my hoof took me to a small butterfly shell. It had two oval sides attached together. They were red on the outside and faded to pink in the middle. The two sides looked exactly the same, like mirror images of each other.

"I think this is the one," I whispered.

"Adventure time!" Echo said. "I can't wait to see what happens."

I took the shell in my hooves. I got the most **mer-mazing** feeling of warm, tingly **BUBBLES** going from my tail to my horn. That's the feeling of magic!

"I can feel the Shell Sparkle in my scales," I said. "Oh!" A tug on my tail surprised me. I'd never felt that before with any other magic shell.

"What is it?" Ruby asked. "Are you okay?"

I nodded. "Yeah, it's just—"

"Look at your tail!" Flash said. "It's stretching out. Way, way, *waaay* out."

Flash was right. My tail was getting

longer. Pink glitter came out of the
MULTIPLY Shell until—

Pop!

Another Lucky sprung right out
of me.

"Whoooa," I said. He looked exactly
like me. He had the same purple tail, his
mane was the same length, and his horn
had the same number of swirls. "This is
fin-credible!"

"Hi," the new Lucky said. "I'm Lucky!"

"That's my name too," I said. "Nice
to meet you, Lucky." We both put our
hooves out to shake at exactly the same
time.

Echo laughed. "You two even act the same!"

When our hooves touched, the new Lucky started fading back into me. "Bye!" he said. "Nice meeting you." I felt a whirl in my belly, and then he was gone.

"That shell would be perfect for getting an understudy for the school play," Ruby said. "We'd look and act just like each other." Ruby is the best actress in the whole school. And the best baker too!

Flash dug around in his backpack. "Before we use the MULTIPLY SPARKLE for plays, we need to use it for the pearl hunt. How many **fishies** do we need to join again?"

"Eight," Echo said. "So we need four more players."

"I'm sure this will help," Flash said. He pulled his toy trident out of his backpack. Underneath the prongs was a spot perfect for a shell to fit into.

Flash passed me the trident, and I put the MULTIPLY Shell inside. Even more magic tingles went through my body. Now I just needed to wave the trident and picture exactly what I wanted the Shell Sparkle to do.

I thought back to Echo wishing she

was part of a big dolphin pod. "If we multiply you, Echo, your pod could get bigger instantly." But then my tail drooped. "Although you'll have to be careful not to touch your copies, or they'll fade back into you."

But Echo didn't seem worried. Actually, she was grinning so big her smile practically reached her blowhole.

"With four copies of me, we'll have four new teammates with echolocation," she said. "If we multiply me tonight, my copies will have time to practice using their magic before the Perfect Path Pearl Hunt tomorrow. Then we can find all the pearls, and I'll use mine to show me how to find other lonely dolphins and create one huge pod. I'll never be left out of big pod events again!"

"That sounds good to me," I said. "And once you have new podmates, your copies can fade back into you."

I waved the trident over Echo and pictured four new dolphins who looked exactly like her. Echo's tail stretched just like mine had and more pink glitter came from the shell. Then...

Pop! Pop! Pop! Pop!

Four new Echoes floated in front
of us.

"Hi!" they all said together. "I'm
Echo!"

Then they waved at the same time.
They were perfectly in sync.

With the new Echoes moving so well
together, we would definitely find all the
pearls in the Perfect Path Pearl Hunt.
Echo would have her new giant pod in
no time!

A LOT OF MOUTHS TO FEED

"I'm hungry," the extra Echoes all said at once. It was so weird hearing Echo's voice four different times.

The **Fin-tastic Four** and the four Echo copies had all swam over to Echo's place for a slumber party and echolocation practice. Her house was shaped like a starfish with a room in each arm. We were all crammed in Echo's bedroom. It was a tight squeeze with eight of us.

"I can help with that," Ruby said. SPARKLES burst from her horn that became eight perfect lavender tarts. "Eat up, **every-fishy**!"

The new Echoes each grabbed two tarts and gobbled them down.

"Hey," Flash said. "I think those were for all of us."

But the Echoes didn't seem to care. "I'm still hungry," they all said.

"Give me a minnow," Ruby said. "I need my SPARKLE to recharge."

Taking care of four new dolphins was going to be harder than I thought.

"I think we have some Frosted Fish Flakes in the pantry," Echo said. "I'll be right back."

Frosted Fish Flakes was my most

favorite food in the whole ocean. "I'll help!" I said.

Echo and I swam into the living room at the center of her starfish house. Her dad Dalton was watching DSPN, the Dolphin Sports Programming Network. "What are you up to, Echo?" he asked.

"Just grabbing a snack."

"Don't ruin your appetite," Dalton replied. "We're making Plankton Pizza tonight."

"No problem, Dad." Echo grabbed my hoof and pulled me behind her. When we got to the kitchen, she said, "We got so excited I forgot to tell my dads we were going to use the MULTIPLY Shell SPARKLE. We can't tell them they have four new Echoes to feed now, or else they'll know we used the shell without asking first."

Echo was right. Our parents didn't mind us using Shell SPARKLE as long as we asked first. But I had an idea how we could make it right.

"Don't worry," I said. "We'll take care of them until tomorrow's pearl hunt. Once we get all the Perfect Path Pearls, your copies can fade back into you. Then your dads won't have to take care of four new dolphin daughters."

Echo looked relieved. "Thanks, Lucky. Now let's feed those extra Echoes."

We looked in the pantry, but there was only enough Frosted Fish Flakes left for one bowl.

"I can use the MULTIPLY Shell," I said. "I'll copy the bowl four times so we have enough to feed **every-fishy**."

Crash!

It sounded like something fell in Echo's room.

"Is everything all right?" Dalton called.

We swam out of the kitchen as fast as we could. I was extra careful not to spill the cereal.

"You bet, Dad!" Echo said.

"I'm just a little clumsy," I added. "I trip all the time."

We got to Echo's room and slammed the door shut. It was a *mess!* One Echo was bouncing on the bed, another was pulling out all of Echo's dresser drawers, and the last two were fighting over the toy trident with the MULTIPLY SHELL inside. They must have knocked into Echo's desk because her lamp was broken on the floor.

"We tried to stop them!" Flash said. "But they won't listen. They just keep doing whatever they want. This is so, so, sooo bad, **mermidudes**!"

"I can fix this!" I said. I just had to get the MULTIPLY Shell so I could make enough cereal to keep every Echo happy.

I dashed to the two dolphins fighting over the trident. "Look! Frosted Fish Flakes!"

The two Echoes' eyes went wide. "Finally!" they said. "I'm starving!"

They let go of the trident, and I grabbed it, feeling that warm magic tingle. I waved the trident four times and pictured four bowls of cereal.

Pop! Pop! Pop! Pop! All the bowls appeared in a shower of pink SPARKLES.

"Time to eat," I said. The Echoes all dove for their food. They even chewed and gulped at the same time.

I breathed a sigh of relief. "See. We got this."

"Where are they going to sleep?"

Ruby asked. "I don't think there's enough room for four new beds."

Echo swam into her closet. "I still have my sea snake sleeping bag from our camping trip last year. We can copy that."

She pulled it out, and I copied it with the MULTIPLY Shell in no time.

"Oh, I've got an idea," Flash said. "We should make team jerseys for the pearl hunt!"

Flash found a white T-shirt from the pile of clothes the Echoes had thrown on the floor. With a tingle of magic in my tail and the trident in my hoof,

I copied seven new T-shirts. Then I grabbed my favorite set of markers from my backpack.

"When you're done with your cereal, you can each decorate your own jersey," I told the Echoes.

"Fun!" they all said together.

"That should keep them busy for the rest of the night," Echo said. "Then tomorrow I can teach them how to use their echolocation so we will be ready for the pearl hunt."

Taking care of the Echoes was going to be **easy sea breezy**!

THE TROUBLESOME TWO

Echo shook me awake the next morning. "Echo 2 and 3 are gone!"

I practically jumped out of my sleeping bag.

"Oh, blobfish!" I moaned. "Taking care of extra Echoes is *not* going to be **easy sea breezy!**"

Things had been going so well. Last

night, we kept all the Echoes busy decorating jerseys for the pearl hunt. Echo gave each of her copies a number—she was number 1, of course—and let them draw sharks and mermaids and sea dragons all over their shirts. We all had so much fun!

We even went to bed without any fights over who slept where. But now two sleeping bags were empty.

"We've got to find them," Echo said, frowning.

We poked our heads out her bedroom door. We couldn't hear **any-fishy**. That must mean Dalton and Phineas hadn't

seen Echo 2 or 3 swimming around. If they had, they definitely would have come to ask who these identical dolphins were.

"I'll watch over Echo 4 and 5 when you go find the others," Ruby said. "We can't have them leaving too."

Flash stretched out his tail like he does before he's about to use his superspeed. "And I'll zoom around town to see if I can find the others. See you soon!" He sped out of the room in a blur.

Ruby looked at Echo 4 and 5. "Hmm... How will we keep you two busy?"

"I know!" I said. The first thing I did every morning was brush my teeth. I reached into my backpack and pulled out my toothbrush. The handle was shaped like a mermicorn tail. With a wave of the trident and the MULtIPLY Shell, two extra toothbrushes appeared, and I passed them to Ruby.

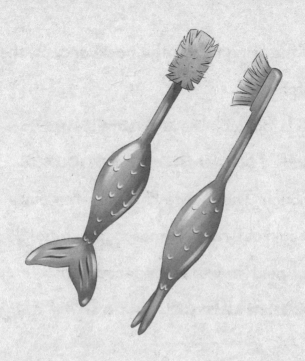

"Okay, Echoes, time to get ready for the day," Ruby said. She led Echo 4 and 5 to the bathroom while Echo and I swam through the house.

Echo used her magical echolocation clicks, but we didn't find **any-fishy** in the living room, the backyard, or the kitchen.

It did look like **some-fishy** had made **seanut Butter pancakes** though. They were Phineas's famous breakfast food. A message in a bottle sat next to plates smeared with **seanut butter**.

Dalton,
Echo and I went to the Mermicorn Island Art Museum.
Don't work too hard.

Love,
Phin

38

"That's weird," I said. "You're not at the art museum with your dad. You're right here."

Echo sighed, a sad **BUBBLE** coming out of her blowhole. "He must have gone with Echo 2 or 3. I guess Pop couldn't tell the difference between me and a copy. We'd better find them so we can win the Perfect Path Pearls this afternoon, and then my copies can fade back into me before they take away all the fun things I should get to do with my dads."

I put a comforting hoof around Echo's shoulder just as Flash raced into the room.

"I found an extra Echo!" he said. "I saw Echo 2 and your dad go into the Sea Glass Library!"

"And Pop left a note saying he went to the art museum with Echo 3," Echo said. "We've got to get them back. I'm just worried Echo 4 and 5 might be too much for Ruby if we leave her alone with them."

"Let's bring them with us," I said. "The **Fin-tastic Four** is stronger together, right?"

I just hoped that the extra Echoes wouldn't cause any more trouble.

BOOKSHELF SHENANIGANS

It took a lot of convincing for Echo 4 and 5 to stop playing with all the **BUBBLES** in the bathtub, but we eventually floated in front of the Sea Glass Library. This was one of my favorite buildings in Mermicorn Island because my mom made it with her magic. She used her BUILDER SPARKLE to mold the glass into the shape of an open book with pages turning and everything.

"This place is **mer-mazing**," Echo said. But she didn't look **mer-mazed**. Her tail was droopy, and I think I saw a tear on her cheek before she wiped her face with a flipper.

"You okay, Echo?" I asked.

"Dad promised he would take me with him the next time he went to the library," she said. "He's been reading about krakens and trying to discover why **no-fishy** has seen one in years. I was supposed to help him."

Dalton is an archaeologist. He goes

on **fin-credible** trips to dig up old
items that give him clues about how sea
creatures used to live.

"We'll get everything back to normal,"
I said. "We'll find Echo 2 and 3, and
after the pearl hunt, you'll be the one

helping your dad on his adventures again."

Echo smiled. "Thanks, Lucky. Let's find Dad and Echo 2, then get to the art museum."

"Come on, Echoes!" Ruby called. **SPARKLES** popped out of her horn and turned into a cupcake. "Follow me!"

"sea-licious!" Echo 4 and 5 said.

Ruby and the real Echo led the way. When we swam inside, my mouth fell open so wide a whale shark could fit in.

"Whoa," I whispered. I had seen this place many times, but I was still **mermazed** by it.

We were in a massive sea glass entry hall. Blue, green, pink, and purple swirls decorated the glass walls. A huge chandelier hung from the ceiling. The arms of the chandelier twisted and turned into **fin-credible** shapes (because she had had help from a narwhal!).

A bunch of bookshelves were just past the entry. They twisted up in spirals from the floor to the ceiling.

"THIS PLACE IS **MER-NIFICENT**!" the extra Echoes screamed together.

"Shhh!" Flash sped over to the Echoes and put a fin over both their mouths.

"You've got to be quiet in libraries. They'll make you shelve books if you're too loud. Trust me, it's no fun."

We turned the corner and saw the most **fin-credible** view. A huge window looked out onto the icy Sea Dragon Trench behind the library. The ice sparkles glinted through the sea glass like stars. It was **sea-utiful**.

But what really caught our attention was who was in front of the window. Dalton floated there with his flipper on Echo 2's shoulder. The real Echo sniffed next to me, and another tear slid down her cheek.

"See what I mean? She gets to share this moment with Dad instead of me," Echo said. "It's nice to have more dolphins with us in the pearl hunt, but my dads can't tell the real me from my copies. I guess things will be better when we win the Perfect Path Pearls and they show me how to find dolphins to add to our pod who don't look exactly like me."

I didn't have time to comfort her because a book fell on my head.

"Ouch!"

I looked up and saw Echo 4 and 5 pulling books from shelves.

"Look at all the shiny spines!" they said. Then they started ripping pages out of the books. "I'm keeping the pretty pictures!"

The Echoes were causing such a mess *and* destroying books! We were going to get in so much trouble.

But Flash thought quick on his fins. He zoomed up to Echo 4 and 5 and tapped them both on the nose. "You're it!" he said, and sprinted out of the library in a burst of magical superspeed.

"Oh no you don't," the Echoes said, then swam after him out the front door.

Flash's timing was perfect because

that's when Dalton peeked around our

bookshelf and found me and the real

Echo floating among the ripped books.

"**oh my goldfish!** What happened

here?" he asked.

While I tried to come up with an

explanation, I saw Ruby over Dalton's shoulder luring Echo 2 out of the library with a cupcake.

"Um, I tried to pull a book down from the top shelf," I said. "It got caught, and I tugged too hard. I'll clean up this mess, I promise. I'm sorry."

Dalton smiled. "These books are really delicate, so I'll put them back. The librarian snail can use her book spine slime to put the pages back together. Just be more careful next time."

Dalton pulled Echo in for a hug. I bet it felt extra nice after seeing

Dalton share the library with Echo 2.

"Thanks, Dad." Echo gave him another squeeze. "We're going to go watch the pearl hunt."

We weren't just going to watch the pearl hunt. We were going to join it. We couldn't tell Dalton or else he'd know we

accidentally used the MULTIPLY Shell without asking.

But before we could get to the hunt, we had to find Echo 3. Hopefully she didn't make as big a mess at the art museum as the other Echoes did in the library!

MUSEUM MESS

Flash gave us a lift with his magical
superspeed, so all seven of us made it to
the art museum in no time.

But when we swam inside the
museum, I didn't get to look at all
the art or dream of having my own
drawings on the walls there someday.
Instead, I had to keep an eye out for

Echo 3. It was extra hard because Flash, Ruby, and I had to keep pulling the other Echoes away from sculptures before they tipped them over.

"These extra Echoes are such a **hoof-ful**," Ruby said as she dragged Echo 5 away from a kelp peace sign.

"We'd better find Echo 3 fast," I said. "Echo, do you think you could find her with your echolocation?"

"Absolutely," she said. She let loose a few clicks and whistles, and then her eyes went wide. "Oh no."

"What is it?" I asked. She looked like she might barf!

But Echo didn't answer. She just sped
forward and said, "Follow me."

Flash, Ruby, and I each grabbed an
extra Echo and swam after her. We
zoomed out of the section with Penguin
Picasso paintings and into the Selkie

Sketches area. These sketches were so cool because they were made with selkie shape-shifting magic. One sketch could turn into all kinds of pictures.

But they looked different today because Echo 3 was drawing all over them with my markers! She must have taken them from my backpack after we used them to decorate the team shirts.

"Cut that out!" I shouted.

Echo 3 looked up, stuck her tongue out, then bolted from the room, running the marker along the wall as she left. We were all so distracted that the other Echoes tugged free and followed her.

"What are we going to do?" Echo asked. "This is not at all what I wanted to happen when I got multiplied to find the Perfect Path Pearls. I just want to find a big pod." She drifted down to the floor and put her head in her flippers. "I didn't want a bunch of copies who cause trouble, or who take the time I was supposed to spend with my dads. This is a disaster, and now we probably won't even be able to enter the pearl hunt. It's all my fault."

"You can say that again," an angry voice said from behind us.

We all turned around to see Echo's dad Phineas floating next to Cindy Clawford. Cindy was the crab curator of the museum. With her clacking claws and glaring eyes, she looked so mad.

"Look what you've done to my **sea-utiful** sketches," Cindy said, pointing at all the marker on the selkie art. "I saw you on the cameras with my own eyestalks!"

Cindy clacked her claws three times. Orange SPARKLES burst from them and drifted to the marker on the sketches and walls. When the SPARKLES hit the marker, it came right off. Soon the room was clean, and I breathed a big sigh of relief.

"You're lucky crabs have Cleaning

SPaRKle, or you'd be in even bigger trouble," Cindy said. "But the four of you are still banned from the art museum for a year!"

"I can't believe you would do something like this, Echo," Phineas said. He looked disappointed. "You're grounded." Then he turned to me, Flash, and Ruby. "The three of you are going to come home with me. I have to call your parents about this."

So much for that sigh of relief. Echo was right. This really was a disaster.

COMING CLEAN ABOUT THE COPIES

None of us said a word while we swam back to Echo's house. I wanted to explain that it was the extra Echoes who ruined the selkie sketches, but I didn't want us to get in trouble for using the MULTIPLY Shell without asking.

"I don't know what's gotten into the

four of you," Phineas said. "You're never like this."

We made it to Echo's starfish-shaped home and swam into the living room.

"Oh my goldfish!" Ruby gasped. "What happened?"

The living room was a mess. The couch was overturned, lamps were on the ground, and the TV was upside down. Prawn Popcorn was all over the floor, and even more marker was all over the walls.

"It must be the extra Echoes," Echo moaned.

"Extra what, now?" Phineas asked.

"We have to tell him," I finally said
to Echo. Her copies had gotten out of
control, and we needed to tell her dad
so we could stop them.

Echo looked at her dad with big
sad eyes. "I just really wanted to join

the pearl hunt. My friends and I used MUltIPLY Shell SParkle to make copies of me so we could enter. We planned to go on the hunt, find the Perfect Path Pearls, and have them show me real dolphins who could be a part of our pod. I was tired of getting left out of so many activities. But now I've just made things worse by creating copies who only cause trouble."

"Oh, honey." Phineas wrapped Echo in a hug. "I know it can be hard to be part of such a small family sometimes. And I'll do whatever I can to make sure you never feel lonely. But you can't use magic without telling me, all right?"

Echo nodded. "I'm sorry. We just got so excited. I won't do it again, and I'll clean up this mess too."

"I think I know the perfect way to help," I said, then swam into Echo's room to get the trident with the MULTIPLY SHELL where I'd left it. When I got back to the living room, I turned to Phineas and asked, "Is it okay if I use the MULTIPLY SHELL to clean up?"

"Thanks for asking, Lucky," Phineas said. "Go for it! We can't let the house look like this forever."

"We'll have this clean in **just a**

minnow," I said, and swam to the living room closet to pull out a vacuum. Then I waved the trident, and three new vacuums appeared in a wave of pink SPARKLES. I gave one each to Echo, Ruby, and Flash. "Whoever vacuums the most popcorn wins!"

Flash won, of course. Using his superspeed to race around the living room, that Prawn Popcorn was gone in a flash.

Next, we had to clean the marker from the walls. Echo found a sponge under the kitchen sink. After I copied it with the MULTIPLY Shell, my friends and I got rid of all the scribbles.

Finally, we put our fins and hooves and flippers together to get the couch, lamps, and TV exactly where they should be.

"We really do make a great team," Ruby said.

"Yeah!" Flash agreed. "We could start a company. The **Fin-tastic Four** Cleaning Crew!"

Echo swam around the living room. "Everything does look great in here. Now we just need to find the extra Echoes."

We sped into all five arms of her starfish house. When we floated into the kitchen without finding a single extra Echo, the real Echo looked like she was going to cry.

"Maybe your echolocation can find them," I suggested.

Echo let out her magical clicks and whistles. She looked in every direction with no luck. "I think they're too far away."

Her tail drooped and brushed against the floor. The motion made a piece of paper float up from the ground. Echo grabbed it and shouted, "That's it!"

She showed us the paper with PERFECT PATH PEARL HUNT on it in big letters.

"They must be going to the pearl hunt after all!" Echo said. "We better get to the Narwhal Adventure Theme Park before they can mess that up too. I mean, as long as that's okay, Pop."

Phineas got one of those grins on his

face that stretched up to his blowhole. "Of course it is. I'm proud of you for making this right. I'll call Dad and tell him to meet us there."

"Hooray!" Flash cheered. Then his eyes popped wide, and he was gone and back in a blur with our team jerseys in his fins. "Let's put these on first. Now we're officially the **Fin-tastic Four** *Copy* Cleaning Crew!"

PEARL HUNT THIEVES

Normally, I'd be super excited to go to the Narwhal Adventure Theme Park. It has the most **mer-mazing** rides made with narwhal TWISTY-TURNY SPARKLE.

But when we swam into the theme park, things were different. **FISHIES** kept pointing and scowling at us.

"Why does **every-fishy** look so mad?" Ruby asked.

"I don't know," Echo said. "But I've got a feeling the extra Echoes have something to do with it."

We saw a big banner over a booth that read PERFECT PATH PEARL HUNT SIGN-UP. A crowd of dolphins and mermicorns and all sorts of sea creatures floated around it. When we swam up, **every-fishy** pointed at Echo and shouted.

"She stole my Selkie Slurpee!"

"She cut in front of me at the roller coasters!"

"She stole the Perfect Path Pearls!"

The extra Echoes had fought over

Flash's toy trident, gobbled down all of

Ruby's baked treats, and destroyed the

selkie sketches. Now they'd stolen the

pearls! They must think anything shiny

or tasty or pretty was theirs for the taking.

"Echo!" Dolly, the dolphin who had announced the pearl hunt at Pufferfish Park, swam forward. "What do you have to say for yourself?"

Phineas and Dalton gently nudged Echo forward. "Go ahead and tell them, honey," Dalton said.

"I'm so sorry, **every-fishy**," Echo said. "I just wanted to be a part of a big family. I let Lucky use MULTIPLY SPARKLE to make copies of myself so we could join the hunt and find the Perfect Path Pearls. I thought they'd

show me how to find real dolphins who could be a part of my pod. But my copies ruined everything. I'll fix this, I promise."

As Echo spoke, all the scowls in the crowd softened. Dolly even hugged Echo.

"Oh, darling, I had no idea you felt left out," Dolly said. "You can always join me and my pod anytime, you hear?"

A tear trailed down Echo's cheek. "You mean it?"

"Of course." Dolly smiled. "And I bet any pod here would love to have you."

Dolphins all around the group nodded. Some even swam forward to join Dolly and Echo, and in no time at all, it was one big dolphin pod hug.

"Thanks, **every-fishy**," Echo said. "Now I need to find my copies and get the pearls back. Did **any-fishy** see where they went?"

That's when a huge yell came from the carnival games section behind the sign-up booth.

We spotted our first extra Echo in front of the **BUBBLE RING TOSS GAME**. Echo 2 had swum into the booth and taken a huge fluffy narwhal doll. The walrus attendant looked really flustered as Echo 2 swam away and popped all the **BUBBLE RINGS** behind her.

"Quick!" Echo shouted. "We've got to catch that dolphin!"

9

BOOTH BOXED IN

The carnival games area was one
of the most **fin-credible** parts of the
Narwhal Adventure Theme Park. There
were dozens of games to choose from
like the **BUBBLE RING TOSS**, the
Guess-How-Many-Guppy-Gummies-
Are-in-a-Jar game, and Shell Skee-Ball.
All the booths had huge stuffed animal

prizes to take home when you won. But Echo 2 had decided to take a shortcut and steal her prize.

"You've got to give that back," Echo said. "You didn't win it."

Echo 2 looked over her shoulder, stuck her tongue out, and took off

around a Sea Dragon Darts booth.

"I don't think she wants to play fair," Ruby said. "How are we going to stop her?"

I remembered the games area of the theme park pretty well because it's where I won *Manta Lisa*, my favorite poster.

"There's only one way out of the carnival games," I said. "If we can get to the exit before Echo 2, we can stop her. And I know of one fishy who is *super speedy.*"

Echo, Ruby, and I turned to Flash.

"Ooh, ooh, ooh!" Flash said. "I know

the answer to this one. It's *me*!
I'm the super-speedy fishy you
know!"

I laughed. "You got that right!
Can you take us to the pathway out
of here? If we all stand together,
we can block Echo 2 before she gets
away."

"Grab on!" Flash said. Ruby and
Echo placed a hoof and a flipper in his
fins. "I'll be back for you in a flash,
Lucky!"

My friends were gone in a blur, but
Flash was back just a few seconds
later. "Sorry that took so long," he said.

"I saw someone with Caramel Coral Candy and I got distracted."

"You think that was long? I must seem like a sea snail compared to you!" I took hold of Flash's fin, and in no time at all the **Fin-tastic Four** was together again.

Echo pointed over my shoulder. "Here she comes!"

Echo 2 floated around the Shell Skee-Ball booth. She had the big fluffy narwhal in one flipper, and two Perfect Path Pearls in the other.

"Let's float shoulder to shoulder," I said. But when my friends drifted next to me, there was still a lot of space for Echo 2 to get by. The path was way bigger than I remembered.

"Are you kidding me?" Echo 2 laughed. "I can get by **easy sea breezy**."

"I'll sprint after her if she tries to get past," Flash said. "Then I'll grab her and wait for Echo, so her copy can meld back into her."

That plan didn't feel quite right to me. "That seems like it could work, but Echo 2 might get hurt if you grab her. We need to think of something that could block her in, then let Echo gently hug her so they drift back together."

That's when I felt a tingle in my tail that told me to get the trident and MULTIPLY Shell from my backpack. Echo 2 was sticking her tongue out at us right next to the Shell Skee-Ball booth. If I multiplied the booth, we could box her in. And Echo's dads said we could use Shell SPARKLE if it helped us find the copies.

"I have an idea," I said. I reached into my backpack and took out the trident. I pictured the booth multiplying, then waved the shell two times. In a shower of pink SPARKLES, two copies of the booth and all its stuffed animals

appeared. They formed a box around
Echo 2.

"Now, Echo! Dive in and hug her."

Echo was almost as fast as Flash.
She dove in past the multiplied
stuffed animals and wrapped Echo 2

up in her flippers. Echo's copy drifted into her right before our eyes. The big stuffed narwhal and Perfect Path Pearls that Echo 2 had fell to the ocean floor.

"That was **fin-credible**!" Flash yelled. "You dove in there so fast! Are you sure you're not part seahorse?"

"Thanks, Flash." Echo reached down and grabbed the pearls. "One down, three to go. Let's find those extra Echoes!"

10

IT'S RAINING PIE

It didn't take long to find the next
Echo copy. We left the games area
and rounded the corner into the
Jellyfish Jumping Pit. It had a bunch of
trampolines shaped like jellyfish that
floated below us. The bouncy parts
were the big round bodies. When you
jumped on them, their tentacles wiggled.

Underneath the floating jellyfish trampolines was a big ball pit. That way if you fell off, you wouldn't get hurt. It was actually really fun to dive into.

But today, **no-fishy** looked like they were having fun. Instead, all the hopping dolphins, mermicorns, mermaids, and selkies looked really angry, and we quickly saw why.

Echo 3 held two Perfect Path Pearls over her head on the highest jellyfish trampoline. Her tongue was stuck out just like Echo 2. Anytime **some-fishy** tried to hop or swim up to her and take the pearls away, she'd push them down into the ball pit.

"She's up so high," Echo said. "We won't be able to sneak up on her because she'll see us coming."

Flash's stomach rumbled. "Food always distracts me from anything.

Based on how many times they said they were hungry, it seems like those extra Echoes sure like to eat, too."

"You're right, Flash!" I said. "Ruby, do you think you could use your BaKiNg SPaRKlE to grab Echo 3's attention? Then Echo can sneak up on her while she's eating and give her a big hug so they'll drift together."

"I'm on it!" Ruby squinted her eyes and wiggled her tail, and then red SPaRKlES burst from her horn. All the glittery light turned into a Parrotfish Peach Pie that was the perfect snack size.

"Hmm," Ruby said, frowning at her

pie. "Echo 3 could probably eat this in two quick bites. I don't know if that will be long enough for a distraction."

I reached inside my backpack and pulled out the MULTIPLY Shell. "Luckily, I think this will help."

I waved the trident back and forth

over and over and over. A ton of pink SPARKLES rushed out of the shell. That warm bubbly feeling of magic went through my tail as Ruby's Parrotfish Peach Pie multiplied. When I stopped waving the trident, *twenty* pies floated in front of us.

Echo's dorsal fin shook. "Lucky, that's just peachy! Grab a **flipper-ful** and let's go!"

We each took five pies and hopped our way up the jellyfish trampolines. I was about to bounce up to Echo 3's jellyfish when the real Echo said, "Wait. We can't just swim up there. She might push us down. But I think I know what to do."

Echo took one of her pies and threw it on our trampoline. It bounced, arced over our heads, then landed perfectly on Echo 3's jellyfish.

"TREATS!" Echo 3 yelled.

"Good one, Echo!" I said, then bounced a pie up too.

"Another one!" Echo 3 called, then gobbled both down in one bite.

"Let's bounce all our pies together so she has too many to eat at once," Echo said. "Ready? One, two, three, BOUNCE!"

We each threw our pies against our

trampoline. They soared up to Echo 3 in
a big baked arc.

"It looks like it's raining pies!"
Flash said.

He was right. It looked so funny that
we all laughed. Even Echo 3. While her

copy was giggling at the pies raining down on her, Echo swam up as fast as she could.

Echo 3's eyes went wide. "Hey!" she said with her mouth full. "What are you—"

But Echo lunged forward and hugged her, making Echo 3 fade away. The pearls and pies in Echo 3's flippers fell to the trampoline. Echo caught the pearls when they bounced back up, then held them high over her head.

"Two Echoes down! Two to go!"

ROLLER-COASTER ROLE

We swam out of the Jellyfish
Jumping Pit and into my favorite
part of the whole Narwhal Adventure
Theme Park: the roller coasters! This
was the part where the narwhals'
TWISTY-TURNY SPARKLE really shined.

"Ooh, ooh, ooh!" Flash jumped up and
down, even without a jellyfish trampoline

under him. "Can we ride the Supersonic Seahorse? Pleeease?"

The Supersonic Seahorse was the fastest roller coaster in all the seven seas. Each seat was shaped like a seahorse. It moved so fast, your lips pulled back! And your mane too!

"I promise we can go for a spin after we find the rest of my copies," Echo said. She let loose a few magical clicks. "My echolocation says the next one should be...*there!*"

We all followed Echo's flipper to see Echo 4 just as she cut in line for the Supersonic Seahorse. She pushed

fishies out of her way and swam in front of them, cutting her way up to the very front.

"I wish the MULTIPLY Shell SPARKle had taught my copies some manners," Echo said.

We watched as Echo 4 took off in a seahorse-shaped roller-coaster car. The ride was so fast that she was back less than a minute later. When other **fishies** tried to take a turn, Echo 4 didn't move. Instead, she just stuck her tongue out.

"Uh-oh," Echo said. "She's causing even more trouble. How are we going to get Echo 4 off the ride?"

"What if we come to her instead?" Flash suggested.

"We need to have something she wants," Ruby said. "All these extra Echoes love treats and toys and shiny pearls. We should bring her a gift! Then, when Echo 4 reaches for it, just gently tap her flipper and *ta-da*! She drifts back into you."

Echo looked suspicious. "I'm not sure it will be that easy. Don't you think she'll swim away if she sees me coming?"

Ruby nodded. "Which is why we need costumes. If only we had my treasure chest full of wigs."

I looked around to find anything we could use as a disguise. That's when I saw a sea dragon selling narwhal hats. They had a big tusk on them, just like our friend Nelia's.

I looked inside my backpack. I had just enough sand dollars from my allowance to buy a hat and a pair of sunglasses.

"Be right back," I said. I dashed forward and paid for the hat and glasses. Then waving the trident and the MULTIPLY SHELL, I made three copies. Now we each had a costume!

"This is perfect," Ruby said, putting on her hat. Echo and Flash did too. "It's your time to shine, Echo. Just pretend to have gifts for Echo 4, and we'll be out of here in no time."

Echo nodded. Her dorsal fin even shook with excitement a little bit. "Got it," she said. "I've never acted before, but this should be fun!"

Echo led the way as we swam up the line. Some **fishies** grumbled that we were cutting, so Echo said, "No cutting here, **every-fishy**. We're on official business."

We made it to the front of the line

just as Echo 4's Supersonic Seahorse car sped into the station. When we approached her, she didn't swim away. The narwhal hat and sunglasses disguise worked! She still stuck her tongue out at us though.

"This is my ride," Echo 4 said. "I'm not budging."

Echo puffed up her chest. "Of course not, ma'am," she said. "We're here because you're the one millionth rider of the Supersonic Seahorse."

Echo 4's dorsal fin shook just like the real Echo's. "I am?"

"Yes," Echo said. "We have a prize

for you to celebrate this very special moment."

Echo 4 looked at Echo's empty flippers. "Where is it?"

"Um…" Echo looked over her shoulder. We had to think fast, and I was the only one carrying something we could give her.

"Oh, here it is!" I said, and I gave Echo my backpack.

When Echo 4 leaned forward to open my bag, the real Echo gently brushed her flipper against her copy's. The two Echoes drifted together, and **every-fishy** waiting in line clapped and whistled when Echo 4 was gone. Sitting at the bottom of her roller coaster car were two Perfect Path Pearls.

"I did it!" Echo cheered.

Ruby beamed at her. "That was the greatest acting I've ever seen. You have to try out for the next play at the Mermicorn Island Theater."

"I will!" Echo said. "But first we have to finish this extra-Echo disappearing act. We've got one more left."

FOOD COURT FINALE

There was only one place left in the Narwhal Adventure Theme Park we hadn't been.

"The food court!" Flash hollered as we swam through all the food sellers. "My absolute most favorite part of the whole place!"

"Looks like it's not just your favorite,"

I said. "Nearly **every-fishy** in Mermicorn Island is here right now."

Dolly and **every-fishy** waiting for us to find the Perfect Path Pearls floated among the coral food stalls. There were Cinnamon Elephant Seal Trunks, Sea Dragon Ice Pops, and Shape-Shifting Selkie Sandwiches. Baxter Beluga from the Beluga Bakery was there selling porpoise-shaped pretzels too.

"It might be hard for me to find Echo 5 in all this," Echo said. "But I'll give it a try."

She took a deep breath and let out a bunch of magical clicks. She turned in every direction while she used her echolocation. The more she searched, the quieter her clicks became. "My magic is drained. I think I used too much when we found Echo 4 on the roller coasters."

Ruby sighed. "And I won't be able to distract her with pies because there's food *everywhere*."

Ruby wasn't kidding. There was food as far as the eye could see.

"Echo 5 is a copy of you," I said, turning to the real Echo. "If there are so many options of things to eat, she'd probably pick the food that you like the best. What's your favorite theme park food in the whole wide ocean?"

Echo's dorsal fin shook just thinking about her favorite treat. "That's easy. Spun Sardine Sugar. It's sticky and soft and savory and sweet!"

"Can you lead us to that stall?" I asked.

"Of course!" she said. "I'd know where it is with or without echolocation!"

We swam through the crowd until we came to a coral stall filled with balls of sugary fluff. It was the Spun Sardine Sugar. They looked like the clouds we had seen once when we went on a class field trip to the surface. The spun sugar came in every color of the rainbow and were in **mer-mazing** cones shaped like mermicorn tails. They had a delicious vanilla-y and salty smell. I could see why Echo loved them so much.

Sure enough, Echo 5 was there, eyeing the candy-colored display. She snatched a cone of Spun Sardine Sugar and slurped it down.

"Hey!" Candy, the mermicorn who
sold the treats, put out her hoof. "You
can't just take that. That costs one sand
dollar."

But like she wasn't listening at all,
Echo 5 grabbed another cone and ate it.

"sea-licious!" she said. Then she reached for a third.

I'd never seen a madder mermicorn than Candy. "Stop!" she cried.

"I've got to get her to meld into me right now!" Echo said. "Or else Echo 5 is going to steal every last cone of candy!"

Echo burst forward. Just before their flippers touched, Echo 5 spotted the real Echo and whipped around. She was going to dash away. Thinking quick on my hooves, I grabbed a cone of Spun Sardine Sugar. Then I took the trident, waved it ten times, and ten copies of the candy appeared. When Echo 5 tried to leave, she swam right into all the fluffy sweets.

The spun sugar was so sticky that Echo 5's flipper stuck to her side.

"Ew, it's icky sticky!" she shouted.

She was so busy trying to unstick herself that Echo was able to touch her copy's tail. The Echoes melded together until the only one left was my friend. She held the last two Perfect Path Pearls up high.

"We did it!" Echo shouted.

Candy put out an angry hoof again. "But I'm still out three cones. **some-fishy** has to pay for those."

"I think I have just the thing," I said. I waved the trident in front of her spun sugar cones, and they all multiplied. Now she had twice as many as she had before!

Candy went from being the angriest mermicorn I'd ever seen to being the happiest. "That works!"

That's when Dolly the dolphin swam forward with Echo's dads close behind. "I'll buy the whole lot, Candy," she said. "To celebrate Echo and her friends saving the pearl hunt. Spun Sardine Sugar for **every-fishy**!"

POD–SITIVELY PERFECT

The whole crowd cheered as Echo gave Dolly the eight Perfect Path Pearls she'd saved from her copies. Flash cheered extra loud when Candy gave him his own cone of Spun Sardine Sugar.

"Great job, honey," Phineas said to Echo.

"We're so proud of you," Dalton added.

"Yes, you saved the whole pearl hunt," Dolly said. "I hope you and your friends join us in the game. It seems like you got a great warm-up searching for the pearls."

Echo shook her head. "It's just the four of us, so I don't think we can enter."

Dolly frowned. "Unfortunately, rules are rules. Groups of eight are required. But next year, I know any pod here would love to have you be a part of their team."

Oh, blobfish. We had gone right back to not having enough teammates.

"I'm so sorry, Echo," I said when Dolly swam away to help pass out more Spun Sardine Sugar. "The MULTIPLY Shell SPARKLE didn't help us after all. Now we can't win the Perfect Path Pearls to show you the perfect way to find more dolphins to be a part of your pod."

"Actually," Echo said, "I've been thinking. I don't think I need a bigger pod after all."

Instead of seeming sad like I thought she'd be, Echo actually looked pretty happy.

"What do you mean?" I asked.

"I'm already a part of the best pod

in the whole ocean." Echo pointed at me, Ruby, and Flash. "You three, right here. You each dove in to help me find the extra Echoes right away. A pod doesn't have to be all dolphins. It just has to be all friends. The **Fin-tastic Four** *is* my pod."

She jumped forward and pulled all of us into a hug.

"We'll always have your fin no matter what," Ruby said.

"And your flippers too!" Flash added.

I gave Echo an extra squeeze. "That's right. **Best fin friends forever.**"

I heard a sniff behind us and saw Dalton and Phineas wiping their eyes.

"You **fishies** are the best kids in the whole seven seas," Dalton said.

Echo swam over to snuggle in between her dads. "And you're the best dads any dolphin could ask for. I love our pod, no matter how small it is."

"I hate to interrupt such a sweet moment," Dolly said, floating up to Echo's family hug. She had the eight Perfect Path Pearls in her flippers, and her smile was almost as bright as the shiny pearls. "But I've thought of the best way for you to be a part of the hunt. The four of you really explored the theme park to find those extra Echoes. I bet you know it so well by now that you're experts. Would you mind finding the perfect places to hide all these pearls? Then the search can begin!"

Echo's dorsal fin shook. "Do you mean it?"

Dolly nodded. "Of course! You can be our official Perfect Path Pearl Planters."

"Ooh, ooh, ooh!" Flash said, raising his

fin. "We're even already wearing official T-shirts! Good thing I had us put on our jerseys, huh?"

Echo laughed and took Flash's fin in her flipper. "My pod and I would love to help. It's like we're archaeologists, but in reverse—we're burying things instead of digging them up. What an adventure!"

With shiny pearls in our flippers, fins, and hooves, the **Fin-tastic Four** got to work. It was a blast. We laughed, rode rides, and ate candy as we hid each pearl.

When I got home and put away the **Multiply Shell**, a note was sitting on top of Poseidon's treasure chest.

LUCKY,

GREAT WORK TRACKING DOWN THE EXTRA

ECHOES AND SAVING THE PEARL HUNT.

WELL DONE!

A VALUABLE LESSON TO LEARN IS

THAT SOMETIMES MAGIC CAN'T

HELP SOLVE OUR PROBLEMS, JUST LIKE THE MULTIPLY SHELL WASN'T ABLE TO MAKE A TEAM FOR THE PEARL HUNT. BUT AS YOUR FRIEND ECHO SO BEAUTIFULLY SAID, THE BOND YOU AND YOUR FRIENDS HAVE IS WHAT'S MOST IMPORTANT. WHEN YOU PUT YOUR MINDS TOGETHER, I'M CONFIDENT YOU CAN FIX ANYTHING.

CHERISH YOUR FRIENDSHIPS AND I PROM-ISE YOU WILL ALWAYS HAVE PLENTY OF MAGIC TO SHARE.

MAGICALLY YOURS,

POSEIDON

Poseidon was right. The MULTIPLY Shell might not have helped like I thought it would, but that was okay. Our day was still pretty magical. Actually, it was pod-sitively perfect!

JASON JUNE is a writer who has always dreamed of being a mermaid. He regularly swims in the lake that he lives on and tells stories to the turtles on the beach. If he could have any kind of Sparkle, it would be Shape-Shifting Sparkle. When he finally gets that mermaid tail, he hopes it's covered in pink scales. You can find out more about Jason June and his books at heyjasonjune.com.